The Mailbox in the Forest

Kyoko Hara

Kazue Takahashi

Museyon
New York

Even though the sun's warm rays were shining down, a cold wind whooshed as Mayu skipped down the road.

"Hey, Grandma. Who lives in that forest?" Mayu asked.

"Do you think there are bears, or raccoons, or other animals?

It'd be nice if there were some fairies in there."

She was holding the children's magazine Grandma had bought for her on their shopping trip. It had a free gift inside.

"No humans live in that forest," Grandma laughed,

"and there aren't any big animals like bears in there, either. But

there might be some small animals and birds."

On the opposite side of the road a thick line of tree branches from the forest was swaying in the cold breeze.

Mayu was in first grade and was staying with her grandparents over the winter holidays.

She lived with her parents in a big apartment building in the city. From her window at home, close to the top floor, she could see the big clump of trees in the distance, near her grandparent's house.

She smiled every time she imagined the forest.

And now she was staying with her grandparents, who lived right next to that forest. She was very excited!

"Thank you for helping me, Mayu," Grandma asked once the pair got home. " Would you check and see if the mail has arrived?"

When she peeked inside the mailbox, Mayu found one envelope and two postcards.

"There's one letter for Grandpa and two postcards for you here."

"Thank you, Mayu."

Grandpa opened the envelope and began to read the letter inside. He smiled.

"Grandpa, does that letter make you happy?"

"It does. It's a letter from my friend. He has a new grandchild.

I have to reply immediately.

Now that I think of it, Mayu, you haven't ever sent me a letter, have you?"

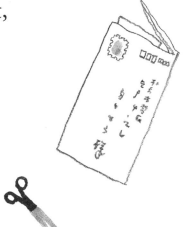

"Well, it's faster just to call you," Mayu replied as her grandfather got out his stationery and pen.

"Ha! That's true. But you can read a letter as many times as you want. And it holds happy memories!"

Grandpa wrote his response to the letter while Mayu worked on her arithmetic homework beside him.

"Mayu, it's almost time for lunch," Grandma called from the kitchen. "Can you come help me?"

"Sure! Oh, yay! It's omurice!" Mayu said.

Mayu had brought her mechanical pencil with her by mistake, so she put it in her pocket and helped set the table.

"Ooh, I love rice omelette!"

"Is it all right if I go explore the forest?" Mayu asked after they had eaten lunch.

"That'll be fine," said Grandpa, "but make sure you go only when it's light out and don't wander too far off." "And remember to dress warmly," added Grandma.

"I will! I'm going to head out now," Mayu said, and put on her coat

Then, filled with excitement, she left for the forest.

Mayu looked right, then she looked left, then she looked right again before crossing the road and heading into the forest.

The leaves on the ground made a nice crunching noise as she walked. She looked up at a big tree and saw a hole close to the top.

I wonder if a squirrel lives up there, thought Mayu. *I wish I could see one.*

She saw birds flying through the trees. Mayu stomped on the dry leaves as she continued through the forest.

When suddenly . . .

Oh? What's this? she thought.

Placed in between two tree trunks

was a box with writing on it that said,

Mailbocks
↑
Please put letters
in here
Everyone is welcome
From forest friend

Mayu tilted her head and looked around.

Forest friend? I wonder who it is?

Grandma said nobody lives in this forest. . . .

Oh! It's supposed to say "mailbox."
They wrote it wrong!

If I'd brought a pencil I cou . . . Aha?
Lucky me!

Mayu had found the mechanical pencil she put in her pocket earlier.

When she searched her further, she found the receipt from her shopping trip with her grandma.

Mayu wrote her letter on the back of the receipt and put it in the mailbox.

That night, every time Mayu thought of the "Mailbocks," she giggled.

I should go back tomorrow, she thought.

The next day, after breakfast, Mayu returned to the forest maibox. A piece of paper stuck out from the mailbox. "To Mayu" was written on it.

A letter for me!?

Mayu quickly looked all around her, but there was no one to be found. All she could hear was the faint chirping of birds.

She grabbed the letter, hurried home, opened it, and read . . .

Dear Mayu,

Thank you for the letter.

Im Konta.

I dont ~~writ~~ write much so my

spel~~ing~~ ling is not good.

Thank you for telling me

I changed it to Mailbox.

Please send more letters.

Your Forest Friend
Konta

Mayu was so happy that she read the letter over and over.

She had never received a letter before. She hadn't written one before either.

"I wonder what kind of kid Konta is. Whoever he is, he's really bad at spelling. He's probably in kindergarten!"

Mayu ripped out the gift that had come with the magazine she and her grandmother had bought the day before—it was a small stationery kit!—and wrote her response.

Dear Konta,

Hello. This is Mayu.

Let me introduce myself.

I live with my papa, mama, and my sister. There's four of us.

My sister is only a baby. She cries a lot, but she is still cute.

I am staying at my grandparents' house right now.

I love omurice and chocolate.

What are your favorite foods?

Do you have sisters or brothers?

Goodbye.   From Mayu

That evening Mayu went to the forest mailbox with her letter.

Her heart beat faster as she put her letter into the box. Then she ran home.

Mayu usually hated getting up early. But the next morning, she woke up at six o'clock and went to check the forest mailbox before breakfast.

As the mailbox came into view, she could see an envelope sticking out.

Mayu hurried over.

"To Mayu." She read the front of the envelope out loud before taking it out of the box and opening it up.

Dear Mayu,

Hello. Thank you for the le~~tter~~ tter.
Its Konta.

My family is me and my mom.
I dont have sibl~~ings~~ing.

My favorite food is chesnuts and apples.

Konta

So, Konta is an only child.

I wonder if he lives close by. It'd be nice to meet him and talk.

Mayu turned and looked around the forest again. It was as silent as it had been before.

Carefully Mayu put Konta's letter into her coat pocket and returned home.

"Grandpa, Grandma, is
it okay to go to the forest to
draw?" Mayu asked later in the
day.

"Of course. Go have fun!
You've really developed an
interest in that forest, haven't
you? Just remember to come
home before dark."

"Okay!" Mayu replied.

She grabbed her sketchbook
and headed out to the forest.

The gentle rays of the sun shone through the branches as Mayu sat down on a stump and drew lots and lots of trees.

After a while, Mayu drew herself and a boy among the trees.

She then took out her stationery kit and wrote back to Konta.

Dear Konta,

I woke up really early today and came to the forest. I was happy to see your letter. Is your mom super nice? My mom is really nice, but she is scary when she is mad. I also like to read books and draw. I drew a picture of us in the forest. Does my drawing look like you? What are your favorite things, Konta? Goodbye.

Mayu

Mayu put her letter and drawing into an envelope and then into the mailbox.

From behind her she heard a rustling sound.

"Who is it?"

When Mayu looked behind her she saw a bird. It let out a small chirp.

Oh, it's just a bird.

Relieved but a little disappointed, Mayu left the forest and went home.

The next day was cold, rainy, and windy all day long.

"Oh my, with this weather you won't be able to go on your walk," Grandpa said.

Mayu had been reading next to her grandmother who was knitting. Mayu looked outside and let out a sigh.

Hmm, I wonder if there is a reply for me at the forest mailbox, she thought. *I wish I could go see.*

Mayu and her grandfather made a
teru teru bozu doll to stop the rain and
bring good weather, and hung it next
to the window.

Through the window, Mayu watched
a bird fly by and head into the forest.

It was still raining the next day.

Mayu and her grandmother made donuts. She was having so much fun that she didn't even noticed that the rain had stopped until she was having her midafternoon snack.

"Yay! I'm going to go out for a short walk! I'll be back soon!"

Mayu left the house and headed straight for the forest.

The forest was a little darker after the rain and there was a moist smell in the air.

Mailbox
↑
Please put letters
in here
Everyone is welcome
From forest friend

The leaves on the ground did not make any sound when she stepped on them.

As Mayu approached the mailbox, she saw that someone was standing in front of it.

Oh, could it be?, she thought.

But as she got closer, whoever had been by the mailbox quickly hid themselves behind the trees.

"Wait! It's me, Mayu. You're Konta, aren't you?" Mayu called out quickly.

"Yes, I'm Konta.
Hello." A nervous
face peeked out from
behind the trees. It was
not a boy; it was a fox
child!

"I know that you all have mailboxes and your homes. It looks like you get mail almost every day, right?"

Mayu nodded.

"So I thought if I made a mailbox, maybe I would get some letters too. I waited for many days, but I didn't get any. Your letter was the first one I got," Konta said happily.

"I see. Hey, Konta. Don't you have any friends?"

Mayu asked, and Konta's face grew very sad.

"The Bears left for the mountains a while back, so we can't play together anymore. The Rabbits moved away to another forest far away."

"Oh . . . Well, you know, I do have a mailbox at my house, but I don't get much mail. That's why getting letters from you has made me so happy."

"Really? Well, here is my reply from the other day."

"Thank you, Konta! It looks like we're friends now. I'll make sure to write you another letter."

Mayu and Konta shook hands.

"Great! I'll be waiting for your letters, Mayu."

Konta looked back
at Mayu several times
before he went back
to the depths of the
forest.

Mayu skipped happily out of the forest. She looked right, then left, and right once more before she crossed the street.

When she was back at her grandparents' house, she opened her letter.

Dear Mayu,

Thank you for the drawing. It made me very happy.

Rainy day's are so ~~booring~~ boaring.

I dont read books but my mom tells me lots of storys.

I like collecting leaves and acorns. Here's a leaf I found.

Konta

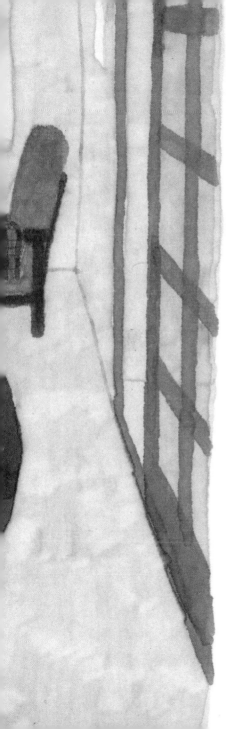

There was a dried, red leaf in the letter. It was definitely a leaf Konta had found in the fall.

After reading the letter one more time, Mayu took the leaf and carefully placed it between the pages of one of her books.

That night Mayu got a call from her mother.

"Mayu, are you feeling lonely over there?" she asked.

"No, I'm fine. I'm having a lot of fun! I made donuts with Grandma, and I've been going to the forest almost every day."

"I'm so glad. Well, tomorrow Papa and I are going to come and pick you up, okay?"

". . . okay," Mayu replied slowly.

"What's the matter? Don't you want to leave?"

"No . . . it's okay."
After her mom hung
up, Mayu got out her
stationery kit and
wrote a letter to
Konta.

Dear Konta,

I have to go back to my house.
The post office doesn't know
about the mailbox in the forest.
I want to keep writing letters
to you. I don't know how we
can do that.

From Mayu

The next morning, Mayu grabbed her letter and headed out to the mailbox in the forest.

I wonder if I'll be able to see Konta again, she thought sadly.

Mayu waited for a while then saw him hurrying toward her.

"Konta?"

There was a bird flying behind him.

"Um, the bird told me that it looked like you were in trouble, Mayu."

"Yeah . . . well. Actually, I have to go back home today," Mayu said in a small voice.

"And we just became friends. I won't be able to bring letters to this mailbox anymore."

"I see. . . . That's a shame,"

Konta said, with his head hanging low.

But suddenly

"Hey, Mayu, is your home far from here?" the bird asked.

"My home?"

Mayu led them to the road. She pointed.

"Look there. You can only see a little of it, but that tall apartment building is my home. I live three floors from the top."

The bird flew off to see.

"That's fine," the bird said. "I can be your mailman!"

"Really?" Mayu and Konta said at the same time.

"Yup. Just make sure to leave some sort of sign for me if you have a letter."

"Hmm, well if I write a letter, I can put a big red ribbon out for you to see," said Mayu.

"Thank you so much, Ms. Bird!"

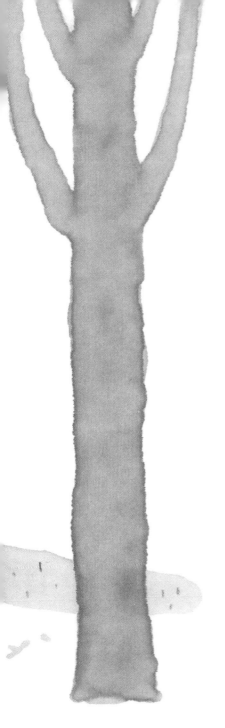

"Konta, I'll make sure to write you lots of letters," Mayu told Konta.

"I'll write to you too. Thank you, Mayu," Konta said

Then the two of them shook with both hands.

That night Mayu's parents, along with her little sister, came to pick her up.

"Mayu it's been so much fun," her Grandpa said. "Please come back during your summer vacation! In the summer the trees will all be green and beautiful."

"And don't forget to call us, so we can hear your happy voice," added her Grandma.

"I will, Grandpa and Grandma, and I'll make sure to come back and visit.

And I'll write you letters sometimes too! Phones are nice, but, you can read a letter as many times as you want, and it holds happy memories inside."

Mayu smiled and she hugged her bag into which she had carefully packed all her letters from Konta.

The Mailbox in the Forest

Mori no Yubin Post
Text copyright © 2019 Kyoko Hara
Illustrations copyright © 2019 Kazue Takahashi
English translation copyright © 2021 Museyon Inc.
All rights reserved.

Library of Congress Cataloging-in-Publication Data

Names: Hara, Kyoko, author. | Takahashi, Kazue, illustrator.
 | Mallia, Alexandrea, translator. | Kaplan, Simone, editor.
Title: The mailbox in the forest / Kyoko Hara ; Kazue Takahashi.
Other titles: Mori no yubin posuto. English
Description: New York : Museyon, 2021. | Series: Forest friends | "First
 published in Japan in 2007 by SOENSHA Publishing Co., Ltd. Renewal
 edition published in 2019 by POPLAR Publishing Co., Ltd." | Audience:
 Ages 4-7. | Audience: Grades K-1.
Identifiers: LCCN 2021008604 | ISBN 9781940842530 (cloth) | ISBN
 9781940842547 (ebook)
Subjects: CYAC: Letters--Fiction. | Friendship--Fiction. | Foxes--Fiction.
 | Forests and forestry--Fiction.
Classification: LCC PZ7.1.H3658 Mai 2021 | DDC [E]--dc23
LC record available at https://lccn.loc.gov/202100860

Published in the United States/Canada by:

Museyon Inc.
333 East 45th Street
New York, NY 10017

Museyon is a registered trademark.
Visit us online at www.museyon.com

English design by EPI Network, Inc.

First published in the United States of America in 2021 by Museyon Inc.
First published in Japan in 2007 by SOENSHA Publishing Co., Ltd.
Renewal edition published in 2019 by POPLAR Publishing Co., Ltd.
English translation rights arranged with POPLAR Publishing Co., Ltd.

Printed in China

ISBN 978-1-940842-53-0

Let's write a letter!